AF415971

EVINCEPUB PUBLISHING

Parijat Extension, Bilaspur, Chhattisgarh 495001
First Published by Evincepub Publishing 2020
Copyright © SHASHIKANT ATHAWALE 2020
All Rights Reserved.
ISBN: 978-93-90197-31-6

7 WAYS

TO CREATE YOUR OWN SUCCESS

The Habits of

Billionaires Mindset

Dr. Shashikant V. Athawale

This book is dedicated to God, to my encouraging parents and wonderful family, and to all my students and the amazing people I have met.

TABLE OF CONTENTS

PREFACE

How this book was written and why

The world is full of strong determined people who let nothing stand in their way. In order to succeed one should have the will to strive, learn and adapt. It takes years of smart decisions- personal, professional and financial to achieve this.

The people who have achieved success weren't born that way. Only through hard work and dedication could they mold their ideas into habits, and then habits into a lifestyle in order to obtain success.

There are no shortcuts. You have to put the work in, so if you're ready to change your life and are up to the challenge, these seven tips will help you. You should start to see changes when you follow these simple habits.

ACKNOWLEDGEMENT

First and foremost, I wish to thank the ever-faithful and unchanging God without whom nothing is possible. He taught me that I am ash and dust. This is a special project, I want to thank my extraordinary family members, who not only encourage me but pray day and night for me.

And finally, I want to thank my readers for allowing me to do what I love.

Dr. Shashikant V. Athawale

Introduction

7 HABITS OF HIGHLY PRODUCTIVE PEOPLE

The Seven Habits of extremely Effective folks embody several of the elemental principles of human effectiveness. These habits are basic; they're primary. They represent the learning of correct principles upon which enduring happiness and success are based largely. However, before we perceive these Seven Habits, we have a tendency to want to grasp our own "paradigms" and the way to create "A Paradigm Shift." Both the Character Ethic and the Temperament Ethic are samples of social paradigms. The word paradigm comes from Greek. It was originally a scientific term, and is used nowadays to mean a model, theory, perception, assumption or frame of reference. It's the manner we are bent to "see" the planet -- not in terms of our sensory system of sight, however in terms of perceiving, understanding, and decoding. For our functions, the easy way to perceive paradigms is to examine them as maps. We've all got a bent to recognize that "the map isn't the territory." A map is solely associate proof of sure aspects of the territory. That is specifically what a paradigm is. It's a theory, an evidence, or model of one thing. Suppose you needed to attain a particular location in central Chicago. A street map of the town would be excellent to facilitate you in reaching your destination. However, suppose you got the incorrect map. Through a printing error, the map tagged "Chicago" was really a map of city. Are you ready to imagine the frustration, the impotency of making an attempt to succeed in your destination? You may work on your behavior you may strive more sturdily, be additionally diligent, double your speed. However, your efforts would solely lead you to obtain the incorrect place quicker. You may work on your perspective -- you may suppose additional absolutely. You continue to not get to the proper place, however maybe you would not even care. Your perspective would be positive, you'd be happy where you were. The purpose is, you'd still be lost. The elemental downside has nothing to do with your behavior or your perspective. It's everything to attempt to with having a wrong map. Then if you have got the proper map of Chicago, then diligence becomes vital, and after you encounter frustrating obstacles on the matter, then perspective will create a true distinction. However the primary and most vital demand is the accuracy of the map. Every person has several, several maps in our head that may be divided into 2 main categories: maps of the manner things are, or realities, and maps of the manner things ought to be, or values. We've got a bent to interpret everything. We have a bent to expertise through these mental maps. We've got a bent to rarely question their accuracy; we're sometimes even unaware that we have them. We've got a bent to merely assume that the manner we see things is the manner they actually are or the manner they must be. And our attitudes and behaviors grow out of these assumptions. The manner we have a bent to see things is the supply of the manner we expect and additionally the manner seem to act. Before going any further, I invite you to associate your own degree of intellect and emotional expertise. Take a few seconds and simply cross-check the image on the subsequent page and thoroughly describe what you see. Do you see a woman? How old do you think she is? What will she look like? What's she wearing? In what quite roles does one see her? You certainly would describe the girl within the second image to be around twenty five years old -- pleasantly beautiful, rather trendy with a petite nose and an overmodest presence. If you were one man you may wish to take her out. If you were in marketing, you may rent her as a mannequin. However, what if I was to inform you that you are wrong? What if I reveal this image is of a lady in her 60s or 70s who appears unhappy, has an immense nose, and isn't any model. She's somebody you virtually certainly would help cross the road. Who's right? Cross-check the image one more time. Are you ready to see the woman? If you cannot, keep making an effort. Are you ready to see her massive hook nose? Her shawl? If you and I were talking face to face, we would've got a bent to discuss the image. You may describe what you see to mine, which I may consult with you regarding what I see. We've got a bent to still communicate till you clearly showed me what you see within the image and that I clearly showed you what I see. Our character, basically, could be a composite of our habits. "Sow an inspiration, reap an action; sow an action, reap a habit; sow a habit, reap a personality; sow a character, reap a destiny," the maxim goes. Habits are powerful factors in our lives. As a result they are consistent, usually unconscious patterns, they perpetually, daily, categorical our character and turn out our effectiveness or ineffectualness. As educator, the nice professional, once said, "Habits are sort of a cable. We have a tendency to weave a strand of it every day and shortly it cannot be broken." I personally don't believe the last a part of his expression. I do know they will be broken. Habits may be learned and unlearned. However I additionally comprehend it is as not a fast fix. It involves a method and an amazing commitment. Those folks who watched the satellite voyage of Phoebus Apollo eleven we have a tendency to be fascinated as we saw the primary men walk on the moon and come to earth. Superlatives like "fantastic" and "incredible" were inadequate to explain those eventful days. However to go there those astronauts virtually had to interrupt out of the tremendous gravitational pull of the world. A lot of energy was spent within the initial jiffy of lift-off, within the initial few miles of travel, than was used over following many days to travel for 1,000,000 miles. Habits, too, have tremendous gravity pull -- most of the people understand or would admit. Breaking deeply imbedded habitual tendencies like procrastination, impatience, cruciality, or stinginess that violate basic principles of human effectiveness involves a resolution and many minor changes in our lives. "Lift off" takes an amazing effort, however once we have a tendency to flee of the gravitational pull, our freedom takes on a full new dimension. Like all natural force, gravity will work with us or against us. The gravity pull of a number of our habits could presently be keeping us from going wherever we would like to travel. However it's the gravity that keeps our world along that keeps the planets in their orbits and our universe as it is. It's a robust force, and if we have a tendency to use it effectively, we will use the gravitational pull of habit to make the cohesiveness and order necessary to ascertain effectiveness in our lives. "Habits": For our use, we'll outline a habit as the intersection of data, skill, and desire. Information on this habit is that the theoretical paradigm, the why and what to do. Ability is the factor of 'if I can do it'. And want is the motivation, the need to try and do it. It could be ineffective in my interactions with my work associates, my spouse, or my youngsters as a result of I perpetually tell them what I feel, however I never very hear them. Unless I acquire correct principles of human interaction, I could not even recognize I want to concentrate. Though I do recognize that so as to act effectively with others I actually ought to hear them, I could not have the ability. I could not knowledge to essentially listen deeply to a different creature. However knowing I want to concentrate and knowing the way to listen isn't enough. Unless I need to concentrate, unless I actually have the will, it will not be a habit in my life. Making a habit needs all 3 dimensions. The being/seeing amendment is an upward method -- being dynamical, seeing, that successively changes being, then forth, as we have a tendency to move in an upward spiral of growth. By functioning on information, skill, and desire, we will break through to new levels of non-public and social effectiveness as we have a tendency to break up recent paradigms that are a supply of pseudo-security for years. It's typically a painful method. It is an amendment that should be driven by a better purpose, by the temperament to subordinate what you're thinking that you wish currently for what you wish later. However this method produces happiness, "the object and style of our existence." Happiness may be outlined as the fruit of the will and talent to sacrifice what we would like currently for what we would like eventually.

————◆————

Chapter One

SET A GOAL

————◆————

There's a saying that sometimes the journey is more beautiful than the destination. That is very much true when it comes to setting goals. Often when we set goals, the most important thing is not to achieve that goal but what we actually do to achieve it. Why do you think the people who set a goal in their life are more successful than people who do not? This is because they strive so hard to achieve it, that they themselves turn their lives around in order to that. They become more disciplined, hardworking and most importantly they focus their thinking, energy in the right way. Setting goal gives a meaning to life, a reason to live and to work, otherwise it would be just a simple, plain, boring routine life which is not at all enjoyable.

In my opinion there are two steps to set goals and to achieve them. They are:

1. Evaluating them.

The only way we can decide what we expect from the future and how we'll achieve it is to know where we are right now and what the satisfaction is right now. So first, we need time to think and evaluate our current situation and then ask this question at every crucial point: Is this OK?

There are two reasons for evaluation. Firstly, it gives us an objective way to look at what we have achieved right now and what we want from life. Secondly, it shows us where we are so we can examine where we need to go. Evaluation gives us a solid foundation to work from.

2. Defining them.

Prioritize these goals or dreams, whatever we want to call them. If there are several then put them in the order in which we will actually try to suffice them. Remember, we always have to move towards achieving them not just setting them.

What are our dreams and goals? Are they not what we already have or what we have accomplished, but what we want. Sometimes we should sit quietly and think through our life values and write them down using a pen and paper. We can get our goals there. They may live right in front of us "on the surface", or they may be deep in our mind lost due to everyone telling us what to do in life.

Think about what really excites you. While alone, quiet; think about those things that really gives us an adrenaline rush. What would we love to do, either for fun or for a living or maybe both? What would we love to achieve? What should be done to achieve success? When the answers to these questions are found, our life will be a little less complicated.

Effective Goal Setting

The purpose of effective goal setting is to realize what you would like in life in a booming, centered and decisive manner by taking the correct actions in a lesser timeframe.

Who does not wish to realize a lot of in less time? Nevertheless, several people abandon their goals before they tend to accomplish them. Why is that?

Some of the explanations include: lack of confidence, not having a viable set up for achieving them, being false by expecting an excessive amount of time, worry of failure, and lastly, excessive amount of pressure on ourselves to accomplish them. Fortunately there are methods and behaviors we are able to adopt for success setting and achieving goals.

How do You Start?

Know that you just value success and accomplishment. Before starting the method of setting goals, grasp that you just merit success which is possible for anyone who puts his/her mind thereto. You want to believe you'll do what you launched to try, to which you possess the skills and talents for doing it. Unless you start with this significant premise, your efforts are going to be defeated and you may be let down of accomplishing what you wish.

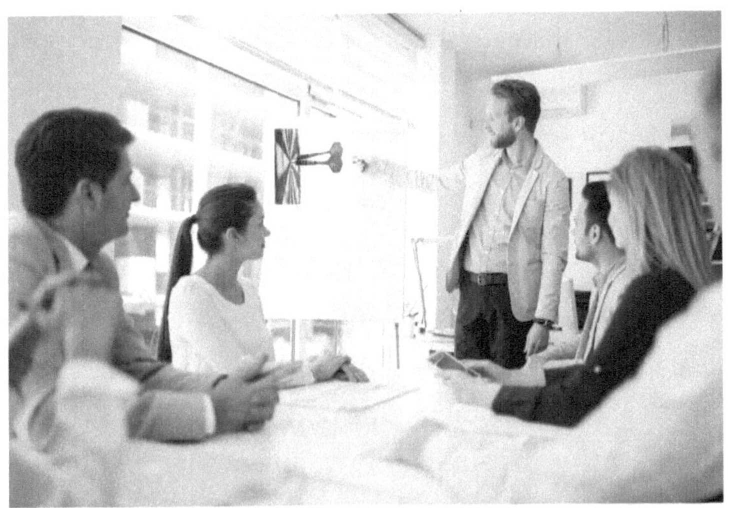

Determine what you want. Hangout with people who are better than you and invest in knowledge. One of the largest issues individuals have in setting goals effectively is that they don't know what they really need. Lacking a transparent idea of what you wish in life makes it tough to proceed. The one factor all roaring individuals have in common is that they're much centered and intensely goal familiarized. They grasp what they require and then they realize it takes setting goals to acquire it.

If asked where you wish to be in five years, you would possibly include: end school degree, be an earning associate, financial gain of x quantity of dollars, have a heavy personal relation, etc. Plan, organize and rate your goals in smaller, manageable chunks. If you check up on everything you wish to acquire all at a time, you would possibly find it intimidating and overwhelming, therefore it is best to prepare and rate your goals. Instead, devise a feasible set up for every item you wish to accomplish. You know that your health goals got to be in the progress ones, therefore establish a daily routine or agenda that you will carry on in an everyday basis.

For career goals, reason them; in monthly, quarterly or yearly chunks. List points, or set up the actions needed to achieve a selected purpose in your career. This might include taking the odd supplemental course, doing further reading, or volunteering within the community so as to implore exposure and knowledge. Since careers take time and energy to create, coming up with and organizing your moves forms judgment. Review, update and revise. Review and update your goals on an everyday basis to confirm they're still relevant to you. Doing this conjointly keeps you on the right track and helps to take suitable steps and actions. If a number of your methods are not operating, fine tune them, or devise new ones. Likewise, understand that obstacles and distractions will be present in your approach and verify what you wish to try to beat them.

We all grasp there will be setbacks and bumps within the road on the way to achieving our goals, however we must not allow them to hinder or lead us astray. Revise and modify the set up how and when you wish to.

Stay centered and intended. Staying centered and intended is perhaps the toughest things to try while setting goals. It's common to sporadically fall off the wagon but it's essential to get back on the right track as quickly as possible.

A great tool for keeping you centered is referring the journal or book you have been maintaining. Re-evaluate it often as an indicator and to remind yourself what you wish to accomplish. Originate routines or habits that may make sure you stay on track.

Other useful techniques for staying intended are to embrace the utilization of relevant affirmations and visualizations. Several roaring individuals, particularly athletes, swear by each of these. It is important to 'see' yourself accomplishing a goal before you really do. Positive affirmations implant positive thoughts into your subconscious mind, that consecutively, prompt you to require the proper actions to realize your goals.

The Benefits of Setting Goals:

1. Gives you the 'big picture' direction you require in your life.
2. Helps to keep you organized and centered.
3. Builds assurance and a way of accomplishment
4. Helps you come through expeditious success in less time.
5. Makes the small day to day tasks more purposeful.
6. Goal setting or positively effective goal setting, has been a tried and true technique for achieving success and accomplishment in life. Without it we might drift from our aim and waste valuable time and energy in pursuits that lead to obscurity.

———◆———

Chapter Two

THEY READ A LOT

Want to understand one habit ultra-successful individuals have in common?

They read. A lot.

In fact, Warren Buffett was once asked what he considered as the key to success, in reply he pointed to a stack of books nearby and said, "Read five hundred pages like this on a daily basis. That is how data works. It builds up, like interest. All of you will be able to have a go at it, however I guarantee not several of you may have a go at it."

Buffett takes this chabit to the acute -- he browses between 600 and one thousand pages per day while he was starting his investment career, and still devotes around eighty p.c. of each day to reading. He is not the only one. Here are examples of some prime business leaders and entrepreneurs who consider reading a serious part of their daily lifestyle:

Bill Gates reads concerning fifty books, which break right down to one per week,

Mark Cuban reads for three hours on a daily basis,

Elon Musk is an obsessive reader and when asked how he learned to create rockets, he answered "I browse books,"

Mark Zuckerberg resolved to browse a book every two weeks throughout 2015,

Oprah Winfrey selects one amongst her favorite books each month for her Book Club members to browse and discuss.

These are not simply isolated examples. A study conducted on 200 rich individuals found that all of them have reading as a pursuit in common.

But these individuals do not simply browse something; they're extremely selective concerning what they browse, opting to be educated over being amused. They believe that books are an entry to learning and data.

In fact, there's a notable distinction between the reading habits of the rich and the not-so-wealthy. Tom Corley, author of wealthy Habits says: The Daily Success Habits of made people, wealthy individuals (annual financial gain of $160,000 or additional and a liquid internet price of $3.2 million-plus) browse for improvement, education, and success. Whereas poor individuals (annual financial gain of $35,000 or less and a liquid internet price of $5,000 or less) browse primarily to be amused.

Successful individuals tend to settle on academic books and publications over novels, tabloids, and magazines. And above all they obsess over biographies and autobiographies of other made individuals for steerage and inspiration.

There are several samples of made individuals throwing in the towel of college or preceding a proper education, however it's clear that they never stop learning, and reading could be a key a part of their success. Or rather, reading is a key part of their success would be more preferable.

Why Should You Read Every day?

The most necessary reason to scan (non-fiction) each day is regular maintenance and updates for your brain. Imagine your body is a piece of hardware and your brain is the organ that runs the package make your body work and the way you expertise life with activities like creating everyday selections to how you are feeling regarding bound things. Reading is a good way for us to connect with humans.

Now here's the awe-inspiring news. By reading, being attentive during lectures, reprimanding folks, being observant, reflective and other alternative things, you'll be able to update your package to be less buggy.

You have the flexibility to create your computer code to be more powerful, more capable, more correct and with fewer bugs. In different words, you become more intelligent once you frequently update and maintain your computer code.

Among all the ways in of "downloading" information to update the "software" that your brain runs, reading is one amongst the most effective and also the preferred one. Reading opens new views and angles to you, it allows you to acquaint yourself with how others see the globe, and it allows you to accumulate skills, improve your communication skills and a lot more. You'll be able to perceive the globe and yourself far better. That's why most of the extraordinarily sure-fire folks, despite the business, browse; and that they read heaps.

Regular reading doesn't solely mean recent updates for your brain; analysis has shown that reading improves your memory and greatly decreases the prospect for psychological illnesses like Alzheimer's. It helps impede your psychological decline with age. Reading is an exercise for your brain. The more you learn, the more junction pinpoints you have got for the new information to be at your disposal quicker and additional for good. Once you scan, you're creating your hardware and computer code extra capable to accumulate the advantages.

By reading books, you'll see into the minds of people and perceive a little fragment of what was/is their knowledge of the planet as well as of those that already gave up the and fortunately determined to share their piece of the planet through the word. By reading, you have the flexibility to enter the minds of people. Don't waste that ability. By understanding other ways of however life may be toughened, grasping completely different angles of viewing different things and having additional information, you develop a fellow feeling. Being sympathetic is one in all the most vital social skills. Reading is the factor that helps you improve your fellow feeling. With a book we can go anywhere and be anything, anytime.

Especially by reading non-fiction books, you'll enter into additional mental states, perceive individuals better and cultivate additional, advanced and deeper relationships.

You'll perceive additional relationship dimensions and be a far better friend. What an impressive advantage of reading!

———◆———

Chapter Three

LISTEN MORE, TALK LESS

People like to speak. If you ever try the exercise of not speaking for one full day, you'll notice that it's terribly, terribly troublesome. The issue expands on the far side the actual fact that you just can't simply raise somebody a glass of water or directions. There's the additional struggle of keeping your mouth shut after you simply wish to allow your 2 cents on a matter, supply recommendation, or maybe unfold gossip. Individuals will focus tons on transmission words and knowledge onto others. For a few reason, we expect it elevates our standing or makes us appear smarter to mention to others. The reality is that, using our language less will really be what makes us stronger. I took up a degree in recent years to become a much better auditor and it modified my life. It has modified tons of my relationships. It created my additional diplomacy in relationships. It even caused me to run aloof from some. Here is what happens after you listen more and speak less.

People who balance speaking and listening are sometimes self-made in handling relationships and are seldom misunderstood. Every word contains a meaning and a price thence they ought to be used cautiously. Useless words solely produce noise. After we use them unwisely, or throw them without an aim to simply grab someone's attention we have a tendency to solely produce a commotion and it doesn't help to facilitate in creating a healthy communication. Talk less, listen a lot more could be a golden rule for a peaceful life. It is therefore said that despite being the sixteenth President of the U.S., Who was thought-about as a high figure lawyer, believed in victimized, condensed communication, although he was a good soul and he never pained his folks. The founding father of Virgin Air, Richard Branson believes in talking less and listening more.

Listen to what someone is saying; listening could be a life ability that helps you avoid misunderstanding. Listening is very important as it prevents mistakes while communicating, after you listen fastidiously it clarifies the message more accurately and may facilitate to cut back the frustration for the speaker. Listening could be an ability that's needed for all sorts of communication. When someone is talking, avoid interrupting verbally. Please keep in mind that where we have a tendency to listen we also have a tendency to keep giving non-verbal feedback through our facial expressions, our actions, our buzzing to the person we ought to be taking note of. When pauses occur within the natural flow of the speech communication, we have a tendency to get impatient and we feel that it's our responsibility to instantly fill the void; which isn't correct. To be honest, we have a tendency to not very hear somebody while they are talking, instead we have a tendency to brood about what to mention next or what we wish to speak. We have a tendency to thirstily sit up for the person's reprehension to end. When somebody asks a matter, will we answer them to the point? A learned and refined person offers little concerning himself to the speech communication. Whereas, most of the people forget that words have power, they need energy as a result of which they vibrate. So, speaking an excessive amount enlarges the facility at intervals and it affects our ability to focus. The more we have a tendency to speak, the more our mind wanders. As a result it becomes progressively tough to regulate our thoughts.

If we glance around carefully, we'll notice that folks who speak less accomplish more; this is often a universal truth. I even have seen that self-made folks are smart listeners and even better speakers. We want to manage ourselves once the urge to talk comes up. We have a tendency to stop it, which could be done solely with apply. God has given us 2 ears and one mouth and that we have the ability to distribute our energies and to use them accordingly; we should listen doubly to the amount we speak. It's better to stay active and keep the ears and mouth magnitude relation in mind.

The folks that are the foremost intelligent are literally those you'd least expect to be good. They with patience sit up for people to mention what they want to mention. They like better to open their ears instead of their mouths. The quietest individuals measure to be the best individuals. They speak less and have good brains. These include the introverts. They're the inventive varieties, the geniuses that get stimulation from learning instead of mingling. They're a bit tough to be noticed: they like to fly below the microwave radar, wordlessly manufacturing the most effective work and also the most unbelievable art.

Every time you have got a language with somebody, speak for 3 to 5 minutes, then permit the opposite person associate in equal quantity of your time to present his/her thoughts. Listen with patience, avoid your sturdy and inevitable want to interrupt the person talking. Rather, develop your skills in asking sensible queries. Also, avoid the one word answer – the affirmative, no, uh-huh, yeah etc. If you can't consider something, take into account the likelihood that you just weren't listening closely enough and work on improving that ability. Develop the habit of backtracking when you had a talk with someone. Recall the sorts of stuff you repeat. Could the stuff you said be phrased another way? Did you overdraw your point? Did you hurt someone unnecessarily? If affirmative, then it's time you should try to be condensed and concision within the words you decide on. The word 'listen' contains equivalent letters that form the word 'silent.'

Benefits of Talking Less

1. We think before speaking

Given time before you speak, you'll place more thought into what you would like to speak to the opposite person. Absorb what he or she is communicating, and use their suggestions to support or counsel your argument. Also, you'll not find yourself communicating on one thing that you probably did not listen.

2. We are able to process what is being spoken

When somebody is talking to you, it's simple to zone out and simply specialize in snippets of what they're speaking. Listen rigorously to them, however they might be talking.

There could also be a degree of underlying issue of which you weren't even aware, the person could also be upset, so you hear them out utterly.

3. We only speak to the context

If you opt to concentrate more, and speak less than you ordinarily would, it'll add up to solely saying what must be mentioned. Why waste some time talking concerning things that don't matter?

If you would like your opinions to create a control, you must keep your points compact. Attempt to create yourself as clear as potential so there's no area for confusion. It absolutely was a man of science who first mentioned, "Speak not however what could profit others or yourself"; avoid trifling speech communication.

4. For Decision making, we have all the info

If you pay attention to your conversations, and you absorb the knowledge given to you, you'll probably have an all-around opinion on the end result of any choices that are created.

For example, if you're in a meeting with many people that have concerns on some specific issue, let everyone have their say before a choice is formed. If you collect all of the facts, you'll be able to build an informed call on the end result.

5. We learn to value opinions of other people

There's nothing more frustrating than gushing your heart on somebody and being met with a brick wall. It's therefore necessary to feel required within the work or home.

If your opinions are valued and brought into thought, you'll feel far better not solely regarding matters, however regarding yourself yet. Turning that around, you ought to make others feel a similar way that their opinions matter which they too, are a valued member of the team.

Conversations ought to be offering and taking. You shouldn't have to be compelled to interrupt somebody to urge your word in. However you shouldn't dismiss what they need to mention either. If you are able to really hear what's being mentioned, method the knowledge, and use it effectively, your communication skills can solely improve as time goes on.

Listening may be a talent that takes diligence and observation. The reality of the matter is that a lot of people aren't excellent listeners. Whereas we tend to take longer taking note of others than utilizing the other kind of communication, listening tends to be a significant a part of communication that we frequently overlook. Specialized listening needs us to be attentive, patient, responsive, and understanding. Once we will do all of those things effectively, then we tend to be more ready to decipher which means, respond effectively, build trust, develop positive relationships, and serve others. There are many things that hinder our listening skills. First, we've trained ourselves to become mindless listeners. We tend to be perpetually bombarded by info and messages throughout our day that we've unconsciously developed a filtering processes. This is often not essentially a nasty issue. We afford each message we receive an ounce of our attention – it'd be exhausting. we tend to simply have to be compelled to bear in mind to take a lot of active listening approach, like id your friend is telling you a conflict or if that person you sit next to in school appears to be having a troublesome day.

Second, there are 1,000,000 very little distractions which will steal our attention. Besides obvious, literal distractions like noise or interruptions, we have a tendency to also produce distractions ourselves. Our own experiences could interfere with or overtake our thoughts. This could inhibit us from being attentive to the opposite person's actual wants. Or perhaps, we're too centered on what to mention next. We have a tendency to get therefore centered on crafting our own excellent response that we fail to actually perceive or understand what others are trying to communicate. People simply need to be detected. Listening in itself is therapeutic. Not solely will listening demonstrate care, however it permits you to grasp what individuals really want. By being attentive to the insufficient details, we can begin to grasp wherever others are returning from.

Chapter Four

FOLLOW YOUR DREAM

———•———

We forever say things like "chase your dreams", "believe in yourself" to ourselves all the time. However once it involves us to put them to a sensible use, most folks find themselves selecting the items that are specifically opposite to our tastes. It's true that life typically interjects and sensible necessity takes over our emotions as a result of that we tend to accept one thing that is different than we had expected. Some even find themself doing employment that doesn't match their style in any means. However, there are some of us that never accept less and break the trend by following their dreams. Believe or not, however there's additionally some science behind on what you are doing. It simply takes the correct place to place this passion so as to derive some which means from it.

Life interjects, bills collect, and typically we've to try and do jobs we don't want to only to simply make it through the day. However, there are a unit variety of reasons to follow your dreams, to interrupt the trend, and to measure the life you've invariably wanted. Why follow your dreams? Here's what following your dreams does:

1. Makes life worth living

Your dreams are what will get you through even the worst days. If you're troubled, your dreams are your reason to stay going. They are why you rise in the morning and check out once more. They're what makes your entire life worth living. Without our dreams, we tend to exist barely.

2. Time goes fast, unlike the boring job which does not end till eternity

Why must you be employed to do something you hate? You'll count the clock, you won't work, and you'll dread rising in the morning.

Instead, pursue your dreams! Get excited regarding your day, and live your life doing what you like.

3. You are happy

Life without dreams is depressing. Search so much and so wide for yours, and build a promise to yourself that you just have to begin following them.

Once you get on the trail towards your goal, you may notice a definite modification in how you feel.

4. Your parents become proud

Sometimes elders don't continually perceive our dreams or they fight to sway us towards a selected one. However, if you're adamant regarding your dreams, and you are working arduously to attain them, they don't have any reason to not be happy with you.

5. You can only live once

Life is brief. Our days are measured, therefore why pay them doing the one thing don't love? It's time to create a call to travel for it.

Dream big. Specialize in your dreams. Create your dreams and make them happen.

6. Dreams and rewards are proportional

The dream you chase can never become a reality and provides you what you're searching for if you don't dream big! Dreams have a part of self-motivation; however that motivation can solely be enough if the dream is of a sufficient size. For example, if your goal is to be a singer, then your dream ought to be to become a worldwide adept and for everybody to understand you're the best at singing. There's no point in having a dream if you don't have the assumption to back it up and understand that you just may be foremost in your endeavor.

Seemingly giant dreams typically attract monumental rewards for those that dare to. If you think that concerning the other, little dreams by themselves deliver mediocre rewards then you get left with a sense of, is this all there is? There is nothing wrong with little dreams however they have to make the idea for one huge overarching dream. I actually have a smaller dream of being sensible at speaking, however it's a part of an overall dream to inspire innumerable individuals worldwide through entrepreneurship and private development.

Have confidence on your own dreams and see if you've got an enormous enough dream. If the result's you don't, then it's time to have confidence it long and arduous, and are available up with one.

7. Nobody is going to follow your dream for you

It sounds funny and it's quite obvious that nobody aside from you have got the facility and favor needed to meet a dream that just you have seen. Dreams would possibly match how much depth and favor that each individual could attach even to an analogous dream, will once more vary. Thus take the initiative and chase your dream while letting others around you chase theirs.

If we can dream it, we are designed to do it

How typically does one dream or aspire? What does one dream of? Why do folks struggle to bear on their dreams? Is it worry of failure, insecurity in their skills or chalk it up to fantasy that holds them back? It has never been detected of anyone dreaming of failure or meaning to be unsuccessful. Failure doesn't play any half in dreaming. It's the dreamer that instills failure, not the dream. It has actually been scanned of the many planned dreamers that failing many times before they intimate success. The distinction is that failure of not reaching to finish their dreams solely inspires them to dream larger.

Many of you fail to hunt your purpose in life and you must. You dream and so follow it up with an inventory of all the explanations why the dream is impossible. You fill your life with excuses and "I cannot." Several nice firms were formed from a dream, nurtured in a small garage or basement and grew to be listed on the big apple exchange. Why not you? Why not your dream? The sole true limits you expertise in life are those that you produce or those you permit others to impose upon you. If you can dream it, you can do it!

Our Dreams are the only things that are Our Own

The most precious issue we've got in our life is our dreams. Your dreams are distinctive to you, and nobody features a dream that's specifically like yours in each manner. Everything you're thinking about, that you've got and what you don't, nothing can last forever. Your life are often summed up with 2 words: "Your Dream." Once all is claimed and done, whether or not you probably did or didn't reach your dream is solely the life of success there's.

Every part of your life and everything you're thinking regarding is indirectly associated with your dream, therefore you better be damn certain to get some clarity on specifically what that dream is!

When you step on the stage to sing or visit the athletic facility to work on your fitness goal, you've got to allow each ounce of feeling and energy that you simply have. You've got to image in your mind each time that this is often your Last Day on Earth which it's currently or never to realize your goal, and feel nice within the moment regarding it. The journey of your dream is simply the journey of your life. It's going to be the toughest issue you ever attempt to reach, and there are going to be times wherever it sounds like your dream isn't meant for you, and it's only too tiring. If your life dream were straightforward, then we would all have achieved our final purpose, and that we would all be flocking to Hawaii to relax on the beach. To allow an informed your dream is to allow an informed life. To allow an informed life is to defy the rationale you got the chance to measure within the 1st place.

How to Actually Achieve your Dream?

Thinking big needs guts. If your dreams are prestigious, many individuals can do and say very little things to discourage you from chasing your potential. The best achievers ought to face this challenge all the time. Learn to ignore it, or contemplate keeping your dreams to yourself.

If you wish to achieve big, strive these tips:

1- Contemplate what is going to happen if you don't think big. You'll regret the items you didn't do way more than the items that you did. Therefore take time and picture however you'll feel if you never even attempt to reach your dreams. Accept how you'll feel if in ten years from now your journey has made you even clearer of your dream life. Generally pain is that the greatest rational motive to really explore your potential. What proportion of pain will you feel if you don't take action today?

2- Be brave enough to let your ability shine. The foremost vital step towards exploring your potential is to understand that you're a lot more artistic than you thinking you are. We all are. Simply watch a toddler play by him- or herself. You continue to have that ability to form together with your mind. However if you're like most adults, you've learned to stifle or ignore it, and to suppress your dreams. Don't, as a result of your imagination may be your greatest strength. Let it run free.

3- Stretch on the far side your comfort. If you're not making yourself even slightly uncomfortable, you're not thinking huge. If one thing appears comfy to you, you're in all probability already doing it. If you're already doing it, it's not getting to take you to the consequent level. That successfully helps to stop you from ever exploring your potential and achieving your dreams. Learning to wear down discomfort is a vital a part of growing. If you've got enough motivation, something is feasible. Learning to lower your discomfort through healthy habits that may be a crucial a part of any upward journey.

4- Its easier than it's ever been. The web and different varieties of mass media have made it easier to travel the world than ever before. All that's needed is success on an area level. That success will then be propagated to different places. Realize how troublesome it would've been to unfold your ideas to different countries fifty years ago.

5- Once exploring your potential, use your emotions as a guide. You'll grasp you're on to one thing once you're engulfed with positive emotions. Keep thinking massive till you come back up with a plan that actually moves you. Then assume even larger and picture how you'll be able to use this concept to style your dream life. If you're like most adults, you've become too logical and sensible. However you're more capable of doing what really excites you than you understand. What does one really need to do? What conjures you?

6- Pay time day by day thinking massive thoughts and dreaming massive dreams. Build a habit to give a couple of minutes every day for turning out with nice ideas. If you have already got your plan, then spend time developing ways which convert your dream life to reality. Keep mapping out your journey and up your set up. Most folks assume too little. We tend to underestimate ourselves. We tend to worry regarding failure. We tend to worry regarding being too fortunate. However the planet desires your massive ideas, and it desires your audacious dreams. You should dream big to explore your full potential, each for your own sake in addition to the worlds. Think massive to measure a life that's fruitful and fulfilling.

Chapter Five

SYNERGY-PERFORMANCE WITH PURPOSE

The very best types of activity focus on the four distinctive human endowments, the motive of win-win, and also the skill of sympathetic communication for the toughest challenges we tend to face in life. What results is sort of miraculous. We tend to produce new alternatives -- ways that weren't there before. Activity is the essence of Principle-Centered Leadership. It's the essence of principle centered parenting. It catalyzes, unifies, and unleashes the best powers on intervals folks. All the habits we've got coated prepare us to form the miracle of activity.

What's synergy? In simple words, it implies that the complete entity is bigger than its elements. It implies the connection that the elements to be compelled to one another may not require any specific work and can already be half done. The remaining half is chiefly a chemical process, and the most empowering, unifying, and also the most enjoyable half. The inventive method is additionally the foremost terrific half as a result of you do not recognize specifically what is going to happen or wherever it's leading. You do not recognize what new dangers and challenges you will find. It takes a huge quantity of internal security to start with the spirit of journey, the spirit of discovery, the spirit of creativeness. No doubt, you've got to get away from the temperature of the base camp and confront a wholly new and unknown geographical region. You become a trailblazer, a scout. You open new potentialities, new territories, new continents, so others will follow. Activity is everyplace in nature. If you plant 2 plants close, the roots commingle and improve the standard of the soil so each plants can grow higher than they would if they were separated. If you set 2 items of wood along, they're going to hold way more burden together rather than individually. The full is bigger than the total of its elements. One and one equals 3 or additional. The challenge is to use the principles of inventive cooperation that we learn from nature in our social interactions. Family life provides several opportunities to look at activity and to apply it. The manner that man and a girl bring a toddler into the world is synergistic. The essence of activity is to price variations -- to respect them, to create on strengths, to catch up on weaknesses. We tend to clearly price the physical variations between men and women, husbands and wives. However what regarding the social, mental, and emotional variations? May these differences not even be sources of new exciting types of life -- creating an atmosphere that's really fulfilling for every person, that nurtures the conceit and self-worth to every, that produces opportunities for every to mature into independence then bit by bit into interdependence? may activity not create a brand new script for the successive generation -- one that's double-geared to service and contribution, and less protecting, less adversarial, less selfish; one that's more open, more giving, and less defensive, protective, and political; to one that's additionally doting, additionally caring, and is a lesser amount possessive and judgmental? Once you communicate synergistically, you merely expand your mind, heart and expressions to new potentialities, new alternatives and new choices. It's going to appear as if you're casting aside a habit, however, you are doing the alternative -- you are fulfilling it. You are not positive once you have interaction in synergistic communication, however, it will appear as if you having an inward sense of pleasure and security and journey, basic cognitive process that will be considerably higher than it absolutely was before, which is the end that you simply had in mind. You start with the idea that parties concerned can gain additional insight, which the joy of that mutual learning and insight can produce a momentum toward additional and additional insights, learning, and growth. Many folks are not intimate to even a moderate degree of activity in their family life or in alternative interactions. They have been trained and written into defensive and protecting communications or into basic cognitive process that life or others cannot be sure. As a result, they're never extremely hospitable to those principles. This represents one in all the good tragedies and wastes in life, as a result this a lot potential remains untapped -- utterly undeveloped and unused. Ineffective carry on every day with unused potential. They expertise activity solely in tiny, peripheral ways in their lives. They will have reminiscences of some uncommon inventive experiences, maybe in athletics, wherever they were concerned in an exceedingly real union for an amount of your time. Or maybe they were in an emergency scenario where folks cooperated to a bizarrely high degree and submerged ego and pride in an attempt to avoid wasting someone's life or to provide an answer to a crisis. To many, such events could seem uncommon, virtually out of character with life, even miraculous. This stuff will be created often, systematically, virtually daily in people's lives. However it needs huge personal security and openness and a spirit of journey. The majority inventive endeavors are somewhat unpredictable. They typically appear ambiguous, haphazard, trial and error. And unless folks have a high tolerance for ambiguity and acquire their security from integrity to principles and inner values they find it redoubtable and ugly to be concerned in extremely inventive enterprises. Their want for structure and certainty is just too high. As lecturer, I even have come back to believe that a lot of actually nice categories oscillate on the terrible fringe of chaos. Activity tests whether or not lecturers and students are very hospitable the principle of the total being bigger than the addition of its components. There are times when neither the teacher nor the coed realize what is going on to happen. In the beginning there is a safe setting that allows folks to be very open and to find out and to pay attention to each other's ideas. Then comes group action where the spirit of analysis is subordinated to the spirit of creativeness, imagination, and intellectual networking. Then associate a degree fully uncommon to development begins to take place. The whole category is reworked with the thrill of a brand new thrust, a new idea, a brand new direction that is laborious to outline, nonetheless it's virtually palpable to the folks concerned. Activity is merely a gaggle together agrees to subordinate previous scripts and to put in writing a brand new one. I will always remember a university category I schooled in leadership philosophy and magnificence. Within the middle of a presentation, one person began to relate some terribly powerful personal experiences that was each emotional and perceptive. A spirit of humility and reverence arrived at the category -- reverence towards this individual and appreciation for his spirit. This spirit became fertile soil for a synergistic and inventive endeavor. Others began to follow this, sharing a number of their experiences and insights and even some of their self-doubts. The spirit of trust and safety prompted several to become extraordinarily open. They ate up every other's insights and ideas and commenced to make an entire new situation on what that category might mean. I used to be deeply concerned with the method. In fact, I used to be virtually enchanted by it as a result it appeared thus witching and inventive. And that I found myself bit by bit loosening up my commitment to the structure of the category and seeking entirely new potentialities. It wasn't simply a flight of fancy; there was a way of maturity and stability and substance that transcended out and away from the previous structure and arrangement. We tend to abandon the previous program, the purchased textbooks, and the presentation plans, and we started new functions and assignments. We tend to became thus excited regarding what was happening that in regarding 3 additional weeks, we all detected an amazing want to share what was happening with others, we set out to put in writing a book containing our learnings and insights on the topic of our study -- principles of leadership. Assignments were modified, new outcomes undertaken, new groups fashioned. Folks worked abundant tougher than they ever would have within the original social system, and for a completely different set of reasons. Out of this expertise emerged an especially distinctive, cohesive, and synergistic culture that didn't just end with the semester. For years, alumni conferences were commanded among members of that category. Even today, a few years later, once we see one another, we tend to quote it and sometimes arrange to describe what happened then and why. One of the fascinating things was that very little time had transpired before there was enough trust to make such activity. I believe it absolutely was a result of the folks being comparatively mature. They were within the final semester of their senior year, and that I suppose they wished over simply another sensible classroom expertise. They were hungry for one thing new and exciting, one thing that they might produce that was actually significant. It absolutely was "a plan whose time had come" for them. Additionally, the chemistry was right. I felt that experiencing activity was more powerful than talking regarding it, that manufacturing one new thing was more significant than merely reading the previous one.

I've conjointly skilled, as I think the general public have, times that were virtually synergistic, times that held on the sting of chaos and for a few reason descended into it. Sadly, folks that are burned by such expertise typically begin their next new experience with failure in mind. They defend themselves against it and cut themselves removed from activity. It's like directors who started new rules and supported the abuses of a couple of folks within a corporation, therefore limiting the liberty and inventive potentialities for several or business partners who imagine the worst eventualities attainable and write them up in legal language, killing the total spirit of creativeness, enterprise, and synergistic risk.

Synergy and Communication

Activity is exciting. Ability is exciting. It's fantastic what openness and communication will manufacture. The chances of improvement are more and therefore real that's why it's well worth to risk what such openness entails.

After World War II, the U.S. commissioned David Lilienthal to go the new 'Atomic Energy Commission'. Lilienthal brought along a bunch of individuals who were highly important -celebrities in their claim -- disciples, as it were, of their own frames of reference.

This cluster of people had a particularly significant agenda, and that they were impatient to work at it. Additionally, the press was pushing them.

But Lilienthal took many weeks to form a high Emotional checking account. He had these people get to understand one another -- their interests, their hopes, their goals, their issues, their backgrounds, their frames of reference, their paradigms. He expedited the type of human interaction that makes an excellent bonding between folks, and he was heavily criticized for taking the time to try to it because it wasn't "efficient."

But cyberspace result was that this cluster became close along, terribly open with every other, terribly artistic, and synergistic. The respect among the members of the commission was therefore high that if there was disagreement, rather than opposition and defense, there was a genuine effort to know. The angle was "If someone of your intelligence and competence and commitment disagrees with me, then there should be one thing to your disagreement that I do not perceive, and that I got to are aware of it. You have a perspective, a frame of reference I want to seem at." Non-protective interaction developed, and an associate degree of uncommon culture was born.

The following diagram illustrates how closely trust is expounded to totally different levels of communication. Very cheap level of communication starting off of low-trust things would be characterized by sensitivity, affectionateness, and infrequently legalistic language, which covers all the bases and spells out qualifiers and therefore the escape clauses within that make things go bitter. Such communication produces solely win-lose or lose-lose situations. It's not effective -- there is not any P/PC Balance -- and it creates reasons to defend and defeat.

The middle position is respectful communication. This is often the amount wherever fairly mature people move. They need respect for different opinions, however they need to avoid the likelihood of ugly confrontations, so that they communicate in a well mannered way however not empathically. They might understand one another intellectually; however they do not deeply investigate the paradigms and assumptions underlying their own opinions and become hospitable to new prospects.

Respectful communication works in freelance things and even in mutually beneficial situations; however the artistic prospects don't seem to be opened. In mutually beneficial things compromise is the position typically taken. Compromise implies that one + one + one = 1/2. Both give and take. The communication is not defensive or protecting or fury or manipulative; it is honest, real and respectful. However it's not artistic or synergistic. It produces a low type of win-win.

Synergy implies that one + one could equal eight, 16, or even 1,600. The synergistic position of high trust produces solutions higher than any originally projected, and each party understands it.

Furthermore, they genuinely fancy the artistic enterprise. A mini-culture is created to satisfy in and of itself. Although it's impermanent, the P/PC Balance is there.

There are some circumstances during which activity might not be possible and no deal is viable. However even in these circumstances, the spirit of sincerely making an attempt can typically end in a more effective compromise.

Negative activity

Seeking the third approach could be a major Paradigm Shift from the divided mentality. However investigate the distinction in results.

How much negative energy is usually spent once folks attempt to solve issues or make selections in association to mutualistic reality? How much quantity of time is spent in confessing different people's sins, politicking, rivalry, social conflict, protecting one's backside, masterminding, and second guessing? It's like attempting to drive down the road with one foot on the gas and also the other foot on the brake. And rather than putting a foot off the brake, most of the people provide it with a lot of gas. They struggle to apply a lot of pressure, a lot of expressive style, a lot of logical information to strengthen their position.

The problem is that extremely dependent folks try to

reach attain mutualistic reality. They are either smitten by borrowing strength from position of power and they go for win-lose or they are smitten by being fashionable to others that they select a lose-win situation.

They may speak of a win-win technique, however they do not really need to listen; they need to manipulate. And activity cannot thrive in this atmosphere.

Insecure folks assume that every one reality ought to be amenable to their paradigms. They have a need to be compelled to clone others, to mildew them over into their own thinking. They do not understand that the strength of the link is in having another purpose of read. Sameness is not oneness; uniformity isn't unity. Unity, or oneness, is complementary, not evenness. Evenness is unproductive...and boring. The essence of activity is to value the differences.

Synergy is important because it helps you work well together in a group. Say you have to make a Prize with your friends. If you synergize, you will be able to share ideas others cannot think of.

Synergizing is about working together to achieve more.

Synergy means to work together to achieve more than two people alone normally could.

There once was a boy. Whenever he worked in a group, he always thought of himself as the best of any of the other members. He would not listen to their ideas and they never got it done quickly enough and the finished part wasn't creative or nice-looking. He decided he wanted to work in a group better.

This is the 6th Habit of the 7 that works to cooperate with others. It is teamwork and optimism in the adventure to finding solutions to problems.

Making a first impression counts, always smile and consider other people's ideas.

Many types of animals have synergy. For example, ants, zebras, tigers. They all work together in different ways.

How can we synergize? Include all people to work together even if they are different and don't know you well. Make them feel welcome in your group.

Synergy is based on differences and similarities. Those who have synergy celebrate their differences and make similarities.

Everyone wants success and an important step to success is identifying the habits that can help us achieve our goal.

Synergy is 6th habit in between below:

Be pre-emptive

Start with the end goal in mind

Make a habit of prioritizing

Always think about a positive outcome

First understand, recollect and reproduce in an effective way.

Synergize

Nowadays, people want quick and simple solutions. When they see a successful person, a team or a group they ask, "How did they do it? How did they get successful?" and ask for their techniques. But these "shortcuts" that we look for, relying on them to save time and effort and also to get the required result, are simply binds that will return temporary solutions; they don't handle the underlying condition.

Covey writes that the way we approach and see the problem is the main problem. We must change ourselves to the core and not just change the exterior which includes our attitudes and behaviors.

By Perceiving and respecting another person's perspective, we have the chance to create synergy, which allows us to discover new options through open mindedness and imaginative creativity.

Synergy is the concept that the combined value and performance of two companies will be greater than the sum of the separate individual parts.

A synergy is where the addition of the parts is less than the whole. In other words, when two or more people or organizations combine their efforts, they can accomplish more together than they can separately. They can get more done working together than they can working apart.

Synergy helps us to form new alternatives and open new prospects. It helps us as a group to make our own new ways and to cast off the old ways.

Once you start practicing these, you can combine your desires with those of another person or group. And then you're not on opposite sides of the problem! You're together on one side, tackling the problem together. What we end up with is both sides getting what they want and they build their relationship in the process. By promoting a spirit of trust and safety, we will prompt others to become more open.

Have the nerve to be open and encourage others to be open in symbolic situations.

Now choose a person.

How are their views different? Put yourself in their shoes for one minute. Does this assist you to understand them better? Now next time you're in a disagreement with that person, try to pin point why they disagree with you. It will help in solving the problem more efficiently.

Jot down an instance where you had great team effort and consider the reasons for such easy partnership or group effort and how those situations could be recreated.

While focusing on yourself along these four parameters, you should also try to be a positive scripter for other people. You must always aspire to inspire others to a better path by letting them know we believe in them, and by encouraging them to take an initiative.

Select one activity for each job that you need to do and pen it down as a goal for the upcoming week. At the end of the week, access your performance. What led to your success or failure to accomplish each goal? Identify a specific activity that lead to failure and improve or sharpen that skill.

Synergy is the benefit that results when two or more agents work together to achieve something either one couldn't have achieved on its own. It's the concept of the whole being greater than its individual parts.

Synergy is often one of the goals of a merger or

acquisition. The two firms combined may be able to achieve higher profitability than either firm could achieve on its own. Synergy can be reflected in increased revenues and/or lower expenses.

For example, a company may acquire a similar firm, allowing it to expand its product offering and, as a result, increase its sales and revenues. This could not have been accomplished had the two firms remained independent.

In management, synergies may be created among management teams, resulting in increased capacity and workflow that was not possible if the teams were working independently.

As for costs, synergies allow for the creation of economies of scale. For example, a merger can reduce multiple levels of management and duplication and spread fixed cost technologies over larger operations.

Synergies may be complicated, but they are one of the most important objectives in business. To acquire synergy will result in more efficiency, more efficacy and higher profitability.

———•———

Chapter Six

THEY HAVE GREAT SELF DISCIPLINE

If you are looking for self discipline control here the ways:

1. Know your weaknesses.

2. Remove temptations.

3. Set clear goals and have an execution plan.

4. Build your self-discipline.

5. Create new habits by keeping it simple.

6. Eat often and healthy.

The five pillars of self-discipline are: Acceptance, Willpower, Hard Work, Industry, and Persistence. If you take the first letter of each word, you get the acronym "A WHIP" — a convenient way to remember them, since many people associate self-discipline with whipping themselves into shape.

Self discipline at the workplace is a positive effort which helps in developing set ways for our thoughts, actions and habits. It is an art of self-control and self -reliance, which empowers a person to stick to his/her decisions and propels the individual towards achieving the set goals.

Personal Management and self-discipline. The quality that I am talking about is the quality of self discipline. It is a habit, a practice, a philosophy and a way of living. All successful men and women are highly disciplined in the important work that they do.

1. Remove temptations. Self control is often easiest when abiding by the old saying, "out of sight, out of mind."

2. Eat regularly and healthily.

3. Don't wait for it to "feel right."

4. Schedule breaks, treats, and rewards for yourself.

5. Forgive yourself and move forward.

It's as if they believe that some people were simply born with divine willpower while others were overlooked as self discipline superpowers were being handed out. The truth is self-discipline is a learned skill, not an innate characteristic.

The definition of sober minded is someone who is serious and sensible. A person who is studious and logical is an example of someone who would be described as sober minded.

Self discipline is the ability you have to control and motivate yourself, stay on track and do what is right. An example of self discipline is when you make sure you get up an hour early before work each day to get to the gym.

Hooray! Let's make a conscious effort to stay self-motivated and spend significant time and effort on setting goals and acting to achieve those goals.

1. Differentiate between ruminating and problem-solving.

2. Give yourself the same advice you'd give to a trusted friend.

3. Label your emotions.

4. Balance your emotions with logic.

5. Practice gratitude.

6. Create a Healthy Mindset.

Self-discipline leads to self-motivation.

1. Set big goals. When you challenge yourself to achieve bigger goals, you really dedicate yourself to the craft. ...

2. Set clear goals. ...

3. Know that every day matters. ...

4. Don't argue with the plan. ...

5. Build a no-matter-what mindset. ...

6. Plan a routine. ...

7. Commit. ...

8. Understand the transformation process.

Simply, self-discipline enables you to think first and act afterwards. Napoleon Hill quoted, "A disciplined mind is a sound mind" and vice versa. The mind is disciplined because it has been subjected to sound principles and judgment over a period of time and therefore thinks differently from many others.

Self discipline is the key to success because it empowers the personality of a person and makes you stand out of the crowds. Self discipline helps in organizing people better as it makes them to get up from sleep at regular times and do things in a systematic manner. It allows concentrating and focusing on your goals.

Self discipline is one of the most important requirements for achieving success, but too often, there is lack of self-discipline. Fear of failure is also a reason for lack of self-discipline. It prevents initiative and perseverance and leads to a lack of inner strength. Temptations weaken self discipline.

Self-discipline is the ability to control yourself and to make yourself work hard or behave in a particular way without needing anyone else to tell **you** what to **do**.

Discipline is defined as a field of study or is training to fix incorrect behavior or create better skills. An example of discipline is literature. An **example of discipline** is a time out for a child who has just pushed his sibling.

1. Start as you mean to go on. Start teaching your kids from an early age about good habits and bad habits. ...

2. There should be rewards and consequences. ...

3. Establish routines. ...

4. Teach them positive learning. ...

5. You'll need rules. ...

6. Give them a process to learn by. ...

7. Engage your kids in activities. ...

8. Tell them they will stumble.

9. Self-motivation leads to success.

10. Self-motivation is the stimulus behind your actions. It is a tool that assists you in achieving your goal and improves your confidence levels.

Ability to do what needs to be done, without influence from other people or situations. People with motivation can find a reason and strength to complete a task, even when it is challenging, without giving up or needing another to encourage them.

1. Give Positivity To Feel Positivity. There's strong evidence that acts of kindness don't just make others happy; they make you feel good as well. ...

2. Focus On What Makes You Happy To Be Alive. ...

3. Look After Your Body. ...

4. Set Aside Specific Time For What You Love. ...

5. Flip Negatives Into Positives.

There are many advantages to self motivated. People who are self motivated for example, tend to be more organized, have good time management skills and more self esteem and confidence. Understanding and developing your self motivation can help **you** to take control of many other aspects of your life.

1. Increase the strength of your focus gradually. ...

2. Create a distraction to-do list. ...

3. Build your willpower. ...

4. Meditate. ...

5. Practice mindfulness throughout the day. ...

6. Exercise (your body). ...

7. Memorize stuff.

What you will gain:

1. Emotional stability. ...

2. Perspective. ...

3. Readiness for change. ...

4. Detachment. ...

5. Strength under stress. ...

6. Preparation for challenges. ...

7. Focus. ...

8. The right attitude toward setbacks.

How to improve self-discipline:

1. Remove temptations. Self control is often easiest when abiding by the old saying, "out of sight, out of mind."...

2. Eat regularly and healthily. ...

3. Don't wait for it to "feel right."...

4. Schedule breaks, treats, and rewards for yourself. ...

5. Forgive yourself and move forward.

Self discipline at the workplace is a positive effort which helps in developing set ways for our thoughts, actions and habits. It is an art of self-control and self-reliance, which empowers a person to stick to his/her decisions and propels the individual towards achieving the set goals.

Discipline is the method used to prevent future behavioral problems in children. The word discipline is defined as imparting knowledge and skill, in other words, to teach. Discipline involves rewards and punishments to teach self-control, increase desirable behaviors and decrease undesirable behaviors.

1. Show and tell. Teach children right from wrong with calm words and actions.

2. Set limits.

3. Give consequences.

4. Hear them out.

5. Give them your attention.

6. Catch them being good.

7. Know when not to respond.

8. Be prepared for trouble.

Additionally,

1. Understand the meaning behind the behavior.

2. Focus on controlling yourself—not your child

3. Be consistent with your expectations.

4. Give attention to the behavior you like—not the behavior you don't.

5. Redirect, redirect, redirect.

6. Exploit the "energy drain."

7. Don't bribe.

How to teach yourself:

1. Look at the big picture.

2. Know the perils of inadequate sleep.

3. Relax already.

4. Do some short bouts of exercise.

5. Get digital self-control support.

6. Know yourself.

Chapter Seven

BE A LIFE LONG STUDENT-CONTINUE TO IMPROVE

As the name suggests, continuous improvement is an ongoing effort to improve products, processes, or services by reducing waste or increasing quality. This continuous effort drives a competitive advantage for organizations that get it right but, as with many things in life, consistency is not easy to achieve.

Continuous improvement business strategy is also known as a continual or continuous process. It's an ongoing process to improve the products, services or processes of an organization. ... The delivery of those processes is in constant evaluation and change, so further improvement can be developed and applied.

Importance of continuous learning and Development of Employees. ... Not only do training programs help employees avoid making mistakes that result from their lack of information and knowledge but they also help the company increase employee retention, gain their loyalty, and ultimately boost organizational productivity.

To streamline work processes and improve workflow, assess the entire operation from top to bottom, looking for areas of improvement.

1. Assess Existing Processes. Look at what you are currently doing with open eyes. ...

2. Analyze Results. ...

3. Prioritize Key Areas of Focus. ...

4. Automate and Streamline. ...

5. Prepare to Adjust.

An improvement strategy is any policy or process within a workplace that helps keep the focus on improving the way things are done on a regular basis. This could be through regular incremental improvement or by focusing on achieving larger goals.

How to Engage Employees through Continuous Improvement

1. Communicate Expectations.

2. Manage Small Improvements.

3. Give Feedback.

4.   Unleash the Potential of your Employees.

5.   Celebrate Innovation.

6.   Promote a Creative Work Environment.

7.   Organize Continuous Improvement Teams.

8.   Reward Improvement.

Training has many benefits for your staff: they acquire new skills, increasing their contribution to the business and building their self-esteem. The training they do can get them to other positions within the organization – positions with better prospects and/or better pay.

How to improve your management.

1.   Select your process. Consider what core processes need to be improved, starting with what bothers you.

2.   Discuss the existing process with your team. ...

3.   Set metrics to measure success. ...

4.   Map out the current process. ...

5.   Get to the bottom of all variants. ...

6.   Review each individual step. ...

7.   Map a new process. ...

8.   Test the reworked process.

Continuous Improvement Manager Tasks:

Drive the improvement of processes and systems in a company, and implement programs that will have long-term benefits. Develop plans, schedules, and budgets for projects to improve existing processes. Supervise and direct the work of CI department staff.

Continuous training is a form of exercise that is performed at one intensity throughout and doesn't involve any rest periods. It typically involves aerobic activities such as running, biking, swimming and rowing. These activities use large muscle groups performing repetitive movements over a prolonged period of time.

Purpose of training:

The purpose of the training and development function is to: Organize and facilitate learning and development. Expedite acquisition of the knowledge, skills, and abilities required for effective job performance.

Among the most widely used tools for continuous improvement is a four-step quality model—the plan-do-check-act (PDCA) Cycle: plan: Identify an opportunity and plan for change. Do: implement the change on a small scale.

Improved employee performance – the employee who receives the necessary training is more capable in their job. ...

A training program allows you to strengthen those skills that each employee needs to improve. A development program brings all employees to a higher level so they all have similar skills and knowledge.

Learners are motivated to learn and develop because they want to: it is a deliberate and voluntary act. Lifelong learning can enhance our understanding of the world around us, provide us with more and better opportunities and improve our quality of life.

Lifelong learning is the "ongoing, voluntary, and self-motivated" pursuit of knowledge for either personal or professional reasons. Therefore, it not only enhances social inclusion, active citizenship, and personal development, but also self-sustainability, as well as competitiveness and employability.

Ways that you can help them achieve this priceless mindset.

1. Encourage Learning Ownership. ...

2. Turn Mistakes into Opportunities. ...

3. Stash a Few Go-To Learning Tools. ...

4. Let Them Take the Teaching Reins. ...

5. Find Time to Play. ...

6. Set Learning Goals. ...

7. Lifelong Learning Skills: Our Gift to Students.

There are many reasons people dedicate their time to increasing their knowledge, both personal and professional, and learning beyond the traditional school years has countless benefits. For the learner focused on their professional life, high among these benefits are: Maintaining and improving skills.

Education to lifelong learner for all Dr. Mahathir Mohamad says, "Education is lifelong process and the people should never stop educating themselves."

Importance of Learning:

Lifelong learning:

It refers to the process of gaining knowledge and learning new skills throughout your life. Many people continue their education for personal development and fulfillment, while others see it as a significant step toward career advancement.

Rules for Engaging Students in Learning Activities

1. Make It Meaningful. While aiming for full engagement, it is essential that students perceive activities as being meaningful. ...

2. Foster a Sense of Competence. ...

3. Provide Autonomy Support. ...

4. Embrace Collaborative Learning. ...

5. Establish Positive Teacher-Student Relationships. ...

6. Promote Mastery Orientations.

Without knowledge, one cannot be successful in life. To grow in one's career, gaining as much knowledge as possible is important.

Knowledge is also very important to shape our personality and perfect our behavior and dealings with people. We need to understand ourselves, our strengths and weaknesses.

What is Life Long learning?

Simply, I believe it is the consistent and deep engagement of the mind and body in the active pursuit of knowledge and experience from birth to death. Now, science is helping to support the importance of learning in keeping brains active and healthy for a lifetime.

Learning a new skill helps you learn things faster over time. By stimulating neurons in the brain, more neural pathways are formed and electrical impulses travel faster across them as you attempt to process new information. The more pathways that are formed, the faster impulses can travel.

Be a student for life. Learning more helps earning more.